When you smile, your bright eyes twinkle

and your nose begins to crinkle.

Your laughter sets my heart aflutter.

Your warm hugs make
me melt like butter.

I love you when you're in a muddle.

Your tears tell me you
need a cuddle.

Your kisses set
me all aglow.

You have the sweetest face I know.